THE VERY ROYAL HOLIDAY

THE VERY ROYAL HOLIDAY

Clémentine Beauvais

Illustrated by Becka Moor

BLOOMSBURY

LONDON OXFORD NEW YORK NEW DELHI SYDNEY

Bloomsbury Publishing, London, Oxford, New York, New Delhi and Sydney

First published in Great Britain in May 2016 by Bloomsbury Publishing Plc
50 Bedford Square, London WC1B 3DP

www.bloomsbury.com

BLOOMSBURY is a registered trademark of Bloomsbury Publishing Plc

Text copyright © Clémentine Beauvais 2016
Illustrations copyright © Becka Moor 2016

The moral rights of the author and illustrator have been asserted

A CIP catalogue record for this book is available from the British Library

ISBN 978 1 4088 6394 7

FSC
www.fsc.org
MIX
Paper from
responsible sources
FSC® C020471

Printed and bound in Great Britain by CPI Group (UK) Ltd, Croydon CR0 4YY

1 3 5 7 9 10 8 6 4 2

To Queen Ellen and Prince Timino ~ C.B.
For Karen and Matt ~ B.M.

The story so far …

BRITLAND BLATHER

KING STEVE DOES SOMETHING SUCCESSFULLY

For the first time in his life, the King of Britland has done something successfully. 'To the astonishment, to be honest, of all of us,' a spokesperson for the Royal Palace declared, 'King Steve has won the Royal Bake Off organised by his brother, Emperor Sam of Americanada.'

King Steve, it is rumoured, is not yet able to colour in drawings wi he lines, but last week he scored a landmark victory against Emperor Sam.

His apple pie was described by Americanadian journalists as 'just awesome', 'totally amazing' and 'super fabulous', which in Britlander might be translated as 'rather good'.

King Steve seems to be on a winning streak these days, since, according to an official statement from the palace, he also managed to button up his shirt without missing any holes this morning.

It is understood that young Prince Pepino and his friends Anna and Holly Burnbright were helpers in the Royal Bake Off, although, as King

Steve was quick to point out, 'I did it all on my own. They just brought me the ingredients. They weren't even there during the final task.' Indeed, the three children had no hand in King Steve's great victory, since they were saving Americanada from an attack by the Easter Princess and her minions at the time.

The three children, it has emerged, were thanked by Emperor Sam with a rather large amount of money, which they are planning to use to go on a Holy Moly Holiday.

Chapter One

Prince Pepino had always had everything he wanted in life: chocolate brownies at two in the morning, a private cinema in his bedroom, the right to read thrilling children's books and comics instead of doing his maths homework, and a giant sunfish called Dave. Until recently, he had never needed to *work* to get anything he desired.

But now that he had to *work*, and **work**, and **WORK** to get what he wanted most in the world – tickets to the Holy Moly Holiday with Holly and Anna – he was the happiest prince the Royal Palace of Britland had ever seen.

On the day of the Holy Moly Holiday, he got up at four in the morning, had his cereal-and-milk breakfast ice cream and pirouetted around the castle, waking everyone.

'Goodbye, Mummy! Goodbye, Daddy! Goodbye, lovely pets! And goodbye, all the Berties! I'll miss you probably not very much … because I'm going on the coolest holiday in the history of the universe!'

The holiday did indeed sound very cool, and the three children had not stopped thinking about it for one minute since they had spotted the advert for it earlier that summer.

 8

Meanwhile, Holly and Anna were saying goodbye to their mum, who was a little bit worried.

'Have a nice trip, my darlings, but don't get turned into stone again, or tumble down a waterfall, or fall off a tightrope, or get trapped in catacombs, or –'

'Don't worry, Mummy,' said Anna, rolling her eyes. 'This time we won't be in danger! It's just a fun holiday!'

Their mum wiped a tear and gave the girls a photograph of their family from when their dad was still with them.

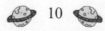

HOLY MOLY HOLIDAY!

This summer, treat yourself to the intergalactic holiday of a lifetime –
Not for the faint-hearted or the unadventurous!

DAY 1: Scuba-dive in the molten lava of the Eyjafjallajökull volcano of Islandia!

DAY 2: Learn to play polo on baby-elephant-back in the savannahs of Afrik!

DAY 3: Build a faster-than-light spaceship in Americanada!

DAY 4: Fly the faster-than-light spaceship to Mars, and have Martian cocktails at a local bar!

DAY 5: Back to Earth! Have a rest and celebrate the end of your Holy Moly Holiday in your ...

TEN STAR HOTEL!

With:

* Taps of hot chocolate, lemonade and chicken soup (unlimited)
* Marshmallow pillows (unlimited)
* Jacuzzi in every room (the size of an Olympic swimming pool)
* TV with three million channels (none of them boring)
* And much more ... including a
BIG, SECRET, SURPRISE GIFT!

'Daddy would be so proud of you if he hadn't been kidnapped by that pelican all those years ago,' she said.

Then they had a big hug. The girls dragged their suitcase all the way down to Doverport harbour, where they met Pepino, and they took a little boat to the Neitherherenortherelands.

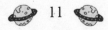

There, the Holy Moly Holiday's special cruise ship was due to leave at midday, to sail to Islandia.

They had packed all the stuff you need for a week-long holiday of that kind. Well, Holly and Anna had.

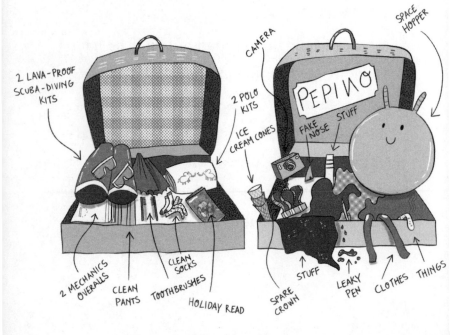

2 LAVA-PROOF SCUBA-DIVING KITS

CAMERA

2 POLO KITS

ICE CREAM CONES

SPACE HOPPER

PEPINO

FAKE NOSE

STUFF

2 MECHANICS OVERALLS

CLEAN PANTS

TOOTHBRUSHES

CLEAN SOCKS

HOLIDAY READ

SPARE CROWN

STUFF

LEAKY PEN

CLOTHES

THINGS

As they approached the harbour in the Neitherherenortherelands, Pepino exclaimed, 'Look at that huge pink-and-purple-and-glittery cruise ship!'

'It's ours!' Anna marvelled. 'It says *Holy Moly Holiday* in big letters on the side. And it's got *swings* on the top deck!'

'Ah!!!' Pepino screamed. 'I can't wait! I can't wait, I can't wait, I can't wait!'

And he began singing 'Can't wait' to the tune of 'Twinkle, twinkle, little star':

'Can't wait, can't wait, can't wait, can't
Wait, can't wait, can't wait, can't wait.'

They all jumped from the small boat to the pier.

'Pepino,' Anna interrupted, 'you're destroying the inside of my ears.'

'You just don't recognise good music when you hear it,' replied Pepino.

'We do,' said Holly, 'and it's nothing like *yours*. It's a bit more like … well, like … *this*.'

This was the most entrancing, fluid, charming tune they had ever heard, played on a stringed

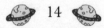

instrument that sounded like it had been made from enchanted wood and the hair of angels.

As they looked around to see where the music was coming from, the warmest voice in the world whispered, 'You won't have to *wait* for long, Your Majesty. Welcome, dear children, to the utterly mesmerising Holy Moly Holiday.'

Anna, Holly and Pepino gaped. The man who had just spoken was one of the most handsome and lovely people they had ever seen. He had perfectly blond hair like a lemon meringue. He had eyes like violet-flavoured boiled sweets.

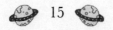

And he was playing the song of the clouds and the flowers on his wooden mandolin …

'My name is Pip Hamelin,' said the man, smiling, 'the organiser of the Holy Moly Holiday. You must be Prince Pepino, and the brave Holly and Anna Burnbright. What an honour. Ready to go? You're the last to get on board. We're lifting the anchor in ten minutes, and tomorrow morning

 16

we'll be in Islandia for the first stop of our
holiday.'

Holly, Anna and Pepino nodded. All they
wanted was to follow this entrancing man.
So they followed him into the huge pink-and-
purple-and-glittery cruise ship marked *Holy Moly
Holiday*, smiling like three happy baboons.

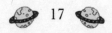

Chapter Two

On the boat, they were greeted by their new Holy Moly Holiday friends. Well, 'greeted' is perhaps not the right word.

'My oh my!' said a shrill voice. 'We've got *commoners* among us!'

'Maybe they're here to wash our clothes!' said another voice.

'Or clip our nails!' said a third.

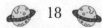

'Or brush our teeth!' said a fourth.

'Maybe they're here to polish our crowns!' said the first shrill voice again. 'Oh! But of course, they're *Pepino's* new friends … I've seen them in the papers. Pitiful Pepino can't find royal friends, so he's had to bend down and pick up some non-royals from the mud.'

Anna and Holly stared in astonishment: the other thirty children who were taking part in the Holy Moly Holiday were *all* princes and princesses, dukelings and duchesses, tsarinas and emperorlets.

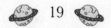

'Bl-Bl-Blastula,' Pepino stammered to the young royal lady standing in front of them all. 'What a lovely s-surprise …'

'*Baroness* Blastula,' said the strident girl to Holly and Anna. 'You can call me Your Highness. I'm Pepino's cousin a few times removed. We all hate him because he's a loser. *We* is me here and them over there: Emperorlet Ursul of Quebecque and Tsarina Nadya of Marok and Mini-Emir Muskar of Syldavia and Princess Petunia of Phrygistan and Count Quetzal of Azteca and his cousin the

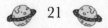

Empressette Zorrina of Chilentina and behind there is Duchess Flora of Florenz –'

Blastula continued to introduce everyone. Holly, Anna and Pepino looked like this:

'– and Archidukelet Ichabod of Atlantis,' Blastula finished – and she took a *big* breath to replace all the air she'd used introducing everyone. 'Anyway, I hear you had to *work* to buy tickets for this holiday. How *bizarre*! I just asked Mum and Dad, and they yawned and signed me a cheque.'

All the royal children smirked. Anna muttered, 'Pepino, do you want *me* to give her a kung-fu kick in the crown, or will you do it yourself?'

But before they could get to a decision, the lovely music started again …

'There shall be no kung-fu kicks on this trip,'

said **Pip Hamelin's** melodious voice. 'Look around you, children: the boat is full of noises … strange sounds and sweet melodies that make you feel good and at peace with the world. Enjoy!'

Suddenly pacified by the mandolin, the children drifted apart and explored the boat in a trancelike state …

And what they discovered was a place of endless marvels – and they spent the next *twelve hours* playing.

SPLOSH! They swam in the outdoor swimming pool for *two hours*. The swimming pool was at the front of the cruise ship and it had ten diving boards, six twirling slides and three wave machines.

SLURP! They spent *one and a half hours* dipping strawberries, gooseberries, plums, marshmallows, fudge cubes, nougat sticks and dozens of different sweets in the giant chocolate fountain. At the end, they just drank directly from it because it was easier.

RRROOOOOWL! The next *two and a half hours* were spent roller-derbying in the huge rink on the third deck. Every ten minutes, an avalanche of confetti fell on to them. Every hour, it was a cloud of foam. All Rollerblades were fitted with little engines and spat fire from the back.

MIAOW! To wind down, they went to the kitten parlour for *two hours*. They had fizzy drinks and ate ice cream right off the scoop, and rested in plush armchairs, stroking and playing with tiny kittens, who purred as loudly as hairdryers and were softer than cotton wool.

SWING! They stayed for *an hour* on the outdoor swings at the very top of the boat. It was night-time now, and the swings, which were entirely self-pushing, went so high that Holly worried they might hit a star.

ROAAAR! For the next *three hours*, they got lost in the dark jungle on the lowest deck of the ship. Shiny fireflies showed them the way to the plumpest tropical fruits, and they played with the funny monkeys, avoiding yellow-eyed leopards …

Finally, at midnight, exhausted, delighted and enchanted, Holly, Anna and Pepino fell asleep in their huge cabin to the sound of Hamelin's mandolin, which was playing through all the loudspeakers in the boat.

Chapter Three

The next morning, after a lie-in until eleven, watching cartoons on the floor-to-ceiling TV screen while having breakfast in bed, Holly, Anna and Pepino went down to the main deck to see if they'd arrived in Islandia.

They hadn't.

'We're still in the middle of the ocean!' Anna exclaimed. 'Not a strip of land in sight.'

'Oh, look! A blue whale!' said Pepino.

They watched the whales around the boat spitting geysers of water, slamming their fins on the surface and pirouetting in the air like gymnasts.

'Are we the first ones up?'
Anna suddenly wondered.
'The rest of them are even lazier than
we are!'

'Holy moly! Don't worry about being lazy,'
said Hamelin's delicious voice behind them.
'This is a holiday. You're allowed to be lazy.'

'Why are we not in Islandia yet?' Holly
asked, turning to him.

'Islandia is very far,' replied

Hamelin. 'But don't worry – enjoy
yourself. Have you had a go at the racing car
track on deck seven yet?'

'Racing car track ...' Pepino repeated
dreamily.

'Are you sure we're going in the
right direction?' Anna wondered.

'Straight to the right place. We're just
taking our time,' smiled Hamelin. 'Off you go.
Play, have fun, enjoy!'

One by one, the other royal children trickled out of bed and into the different chambers, rooms, corridors and secret passages of the boat. Every time, they found yet more things to do, more things to eat, more things to see and more things to marvel at.

And so busy were they that they didn't have the time or the will to fight with one another. Baroness Blastula was almost polite to Pepino when he won against her in the racing car competition. She just drifted away with Ursul and Quetzal, joking about the race and dancing to Hamelin's music.

It was very tiring doing all these activities. Whenever it got a bit too much for everyone, Pip Hamelin would gather the Holy Moly Holiday participants in a circle, take out his mandolin and play lovely songs to them:

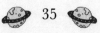

Once there was a singer magical:
He was young and blond and good;
His singing light and musical
Softened ev'n the darkest mood;
On top of all that made him nice
He had the strange ability
To play with such agility
That he entranced ants, frogs and mice,
Flamingos and platypuses,
Carpenters, oysters, walruses,
Corals, mushrooms and cactuses,
And children, kings and princesses.

 36

The singer wanted as his spouse
A damsel of a royal house;
Such was her dearest wish also,
Though her royal daddy said no.

'Quite right,' interrupted Blastula. 'Too many commoners end up marrying royalty. It happened in Francia last week. Revolting.'

Hamelin continued:

One day a zillion ugly Things
(Like ratty kinds of butterfly)

Hatched from the ground – no one knows why!
All that were stung by a Thing's sting
Would die coughing and spluttering.
In the midst of all this dying
The Kings and Queens and Emperors crying
Implored our singer so skilled
To rid the Earth of those that killed.
'O dear friend, lead those Things away!
Lead them to the edge of the sky
And push them off and let them fly
Into the empty Milky Way.'
'I will,' he said, 'only if after

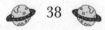

You let me marry my lover.'
'Yes, yes, we will – we'll let you wed!'

('Disgusting blackmail!' went Blastula.)

So he began to sing his tune;
In just one morn and afternoon
The Things followed him, and he led
Them up into the starry skies
Where they fell up and disappeared
With flaps of wings and screechy cries
And never more on Earth were feared.

'Phew! I'm glad the story ended well,' Pepino sighed.

'How did he lead them into the skies?' Anna asked. 'Did he go up a ladder or something? How come they couldn't come back?'

'Holy moly! So many questions.' Hamelin smiled. 'Just relax and enjoy the story.'

And so the day passed by.

Well … perhaps a bit more than a day.

'We still haven't arrived in Islandia,' noted Anna idly, as they finished licking the bowl after making an army of little chocolate figurines.

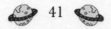 41

The music had stopped a few minutes before, and their heads felt a bit clearer, like they always did when the boat was silent.

'We're getting close,' suggested Holly. 'Look at the icebergs! The sea's looking like Pepino's glass of lemonade yesterday with all that ice.'

'That was excellent lemonade,' said Pepino.

'We should have arrived by now! What time is it?' asked Anna.

'The clock says seven,' said Holly, 'and night's falling outside, so it's probably seven at night.'

'It's night *again*?' asked Pepino. 'Hasn't it been

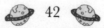 42

night once or twice before?'

They tried to remember how many times it had been dark since they'd got on to the boat.

'It was dark when we played giant chess on the outer deck,' said Anna, 'and then light again as we held those rings for the dolphins to jump through.'

'And then dark again when we trampolined outside,' noted Holly. 'And then dark again when we watched that musical projected on the clouds yesterday.'

'But that wasn't yesterday,' said Pepino. 'There

was a day after that, and then we skated at night on the ice rink and I almost managed not to fall for two whole minutes.'

They listed all of this on paper, and found more to list, and suddenly it dawned on Anna that …

'We've been on this boat for over a *week*!'

'Over a *week*?' Holly repeated. 'How's that possible? We would have noticed!'

'We didn't. Seven days – and this is the eighth night,' said Anna. 'We've been here longer than the *whole* Holy Moly Holiday was supposed to last!'

'How bizarre,' said Pepino. 'I'd have thought Mum and Dad would be worried about us not

 44

coming back. I borrowed their space hopper:
they must be missing it.'

'Come on,' Holly whispered, 'let's try to get
into Pip Hamelin's room. It's the only way to
find out what's going on.'

They put down the little chocolate figurines
they'd been painting (Pepino popped three
or four into his mouth) and they ran up the
staircase to the top deck. Blastula was blowing
bubbles in the giant outdoor Jacuzzi with Nadya
of Marok and Flora of Florenz.

Holly, Anna and Pepino crept up to Pip
Hamelin's cabin.

Hamelin's snores made his cabin door quiver. Only when he slept did he not play the mandolin – and he kept his sleeping to a bare minimum.

'Holly, pass me your glasses!' said Anna. She slipped one of the glasses' arms in the slit alongside the door and – *CLICK!* – flicked the lock open.

They walked in. Hamelin was snoring – *rhoooooppppsh!* – but also humming and whistling to himself.

There was another noise too.

Bzzz … Crrrkkkk … tililit … bzzz …

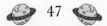

A slice of moonlight through the round window cast a silver light on to the desk, making all kinds of strange instruments glisten: a telescope, a compass, a complicated map, a picture of a beautiful young girl … and a fish bowl containing a buzzing, beeping, bustling electric eel.

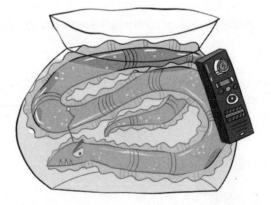

'Look, it's picking up radio waves,' Anna murmured. 'Let's try to tune it.'

She twisted the dials on the fish bowl.

'*Crrrzzzk!*' the fish bowl creaked.

'*Interzzznational news! Bzzzzz … There is zzzztill no … news of the zzzzirty-zzree kidnapped … tüliilit … royal children … bzzzzz … sposed to go on … zzly Moly Holid– sssskkkkrrrr! …*'

'So at least the world knows we've gone missing,' said Pepino.

'*Crrrrr Britlander Royal Family …. grrrzzzspace hopper!*'

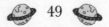

'And they *are* missing that space hopper,' he sighed.

'Poor eel,' Holly said. 'It must be very annoying being used as an antenna.'

'Shush!'

'*Brrrzzzzeeeek … search teams … tlllleeee … been sent to … Afrik …*'

'They've sent search teams to Afrik? That won't help,' said Pepino. 'We haven't even made it to Islandia. I'm not sure we'll ever get to Afrik.'

'*But fffffishermen in Antarktik … spotted a*

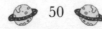 50

crrkkkkkuiseship … some fear … ggrrrrddzzzgg …
children may be heading … towards Southern Edge of
Earthzzzz … tllliiiiiit!'

'The *Southern Edge of Earth*?'

Anna and Holly began to shake.

'What's wrong?' asked Pepino. 'I'm sure that's just a lovely place full of funny, fat, fluffy walruses.'

'Pepino,' said Anna, 'did you ever have a geography lesson?'

'Yes, I learnt to colour in my kingdom.'

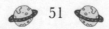

'Well, if you'd learnt to colour in the rest of the Earth, you would have noticed something about the southern part of it!'

'I haven't invaded that part yet,' said Pepino. 'I noticed *that*. What else?'

Anna and Holly rolled their eyes and pointed at a crumpled-up map on the wall of the cabin.

'The Southern Edge,' Holly whispered, 'is where the ocean water has nowhere else to go and just leaks and leaks like a tap into the sky.'

'Awesome!' said Pepino.

'Into the great, big, dark, cold, *empty* sky,' stated Anna. 'If that's where we're going, then it's bad news.'

'Well,' whistled a beautiful, warm voice behind them, 'then I'm afraid, my dears, that it *is* bad news.'

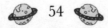

Chapter Four

Pip Hamelin, in his pyjamas, looked like a long silvery eel himself.

'Where are you taking us?' Anna croaked.

'To a Holy Moly Holiday,' smiled Hamelin, and his teeth shone like shards of crystal in the moonlight. 'Have a slice of marzipan.'

'We don't want marzipan! We want to go home!'

'Let me sing you a little song.
Ah! Fair maiden, when shall I ...'

Anna picked up the fishbowl
and – *FLOSH!* – poured
it over Hamelin's head.
The electric eel wrapped
itself smugly around
the singer's neck and
electrocuted him in one
neat shock. *PZZZT!*
Then it leapt out of the window
and into the great icy ocean.

'Quick,' said Holly, 'while he's knocked out, we need to change the course of the ship. I'll try to find the commands – meanwhile, you two go and tell the other kids.'

'I've got a better idea,' Pepino exclaimed. 'Why don't we just escape in a lifeboat and let the other kids fall into the sky? They're all awful anyway!' (He added to himself: 'And then I can have their kingdoms.')

Anna grabbed him by the arm and they ran downstairs.

'Your Bubbly Baroness,' she said to Blastula.

'Get out of this Jacuzzi – we've got important news.'

Blastula was so shocked she coughed into her bubble mix, sending gazillions of prickly soap drops into her friends' eyes. 'How – dare – you talk to *me* like this?'

'Pepino,' groaned Anna, 'get her out of this Jacuzzi.'

Pepino tried to grab Blastula, but she was so slippery she popped right out of his arms, up

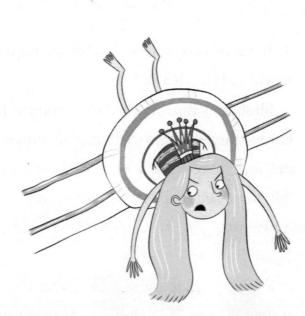

in the air and – *plop!* – got stuck into a round
inflatable life ring that was tied to the railings.

'PEASANT UPRISING!!!' Blastula yelled. 'CALL THE ARMY!!!'

Alerted by the screams, all the other children slowly emerged from various places in the ship – still munching on crêpes or drinking juice out of big golden hat-cups with swirly straws.

'Listen, everyone,' said Anna. 'We've been on this boat for over a week. It's going nowhere. Pip Hamelin has tricked us – he never intended to take us on the Holy Moly Holiday.'

'Who cares! This is better than the Holy Moly Holiday!' exclaimed Ichabod of Atlantis.

'Quite right,' said Blastula. 'There are purple puppies in every bathroom!'

'They'd better be good astropuppies,' said Anna, 'because we're heading straight into *space*! This boat is going to the Southern Edge of the Earth!'

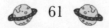

'*Awesome!*' replied all the royal children.

'That's what *I* said,' Pepino agreed.

Anna rolled her eyes. 'Don't you understand? The food won't last forever. If we fall into the skies, we'll quickly run out of things to eat.'

'*Not* awesome,' all the royal children admitted.

'I guess we could eat the kittens and puppies,' mulled Pepino.

Blastula swelled up in anger. *BAM!*

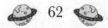 62

The life ring exploded, sending rubber all over the deck.

'We shall eat no kittens or puppies, you cannibals! You're lying, *lying*, because you don't like us having any fun!'

'No,' shouted Holly's voice behind them, from the top deck. 'Look up!'

Everyone stared at the skies above them. And it was quite a sight.

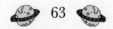

Like a great upside-down waterfall, the ocean poured up into the starry sky, where it swirled into fraying curls of salty water. Flecks of foam fluttered away busily, and the children, even though they were looking *up*, suddenly had a terrifying fear of heights.

'We're going to *fall*,' said Holly. 'Unless we row hard. Down to deck two! I've been through the boat's papers and found how to get the oars out.'

'Me, *rowing*? Who do you take me for, some Oxforth boffin?' Blastula erupted.

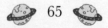

'You'd better come, Blastula, or I'll make you drink a puppy smoothie,' said Anna. 'Hurry up!'

The children ran downstairs to the second deck, where Holly opened a small control box on the wall. A few clicks and beeps later, two rows of fifteen holes opened alongside the flanks of the ship, and oars were locked into place.

'I don't know how to row,' Blastula yawned. 'I was never prisoner of the galleys, unlike some of you here, clearly.'

'Then sit here and hit this drum,' snapped Anna as they all got behind their oars.

 66

'Regularly, and fast, so we row as hard and as constantly as possible! Come on!'

Blastula began to tap the drum. *TAP … TAP … TAP …*

Row … row … row … went the royal children.

(And 'Ow!', 'Ow!', 'Ouch!', 'Argh!' too.)

TAP. TAP. TAP.

Row. Row. Row.

(Blastula was rather enjoying this.)

TAP, TAP, TAP, TAP.

Row, row, row, row, went the children –

('Ouch!', 'Hey!', 'Too fast!', 'Humph!')

TAPTAPTAPTAPTAPTAP.

Rowrowrowrowrow.

'Hey!' Pepino huffed and puffed. 'She's going much too fast!'

'For … once, she's … right!' Anna panted. 'It's the only way to save ourselves!'

'I like your attitude, prisoner number six!'

68

yelled Blastula to Anna. 'Faster! Harder!
Stronger! More –'

But she suddenly stopped, and all of them
did, because the deck was filled with …

… the most beautiful music in the world.

'Why, hello, children,' Hamelin purred,
playing his mandolin. 'I must have

fallen asleep … Holy moly! Why are you rowing so hard?'

All the children shrugged.

'I don't know,' mused Blastula. 'Why are you rowing so hard, everyone?'

'I don't know,' the children whispered. 'It's painful and not nice.'

'It *is* painful and not nice,' said Hamelin approvingly. 'Have some marzipan instead.' Anna struggled. She knew something was wrong, but couldn't say what. They had a good reason to be rowing, surely? But could it be a better

reason than the fun they would have going waterskiing in the artificial mini-lake on deck nine?

She took the slice of marzipan from Hamelin's hand. He was such a nice man! And the way he strummed the strings of his mandolin –

BAM*!* went Blastula's drumstick on the drum as she dreamily dropped it.

This one second of noise, covering Hamelin's music, reminded Anna why they were rowing. The boat was going to fall up into the sky!

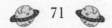

Already she could feel it …

getting to the edgiest edge of the Southern
Edge of the Earth …

and lifting slightly at the prow.

'COVER YOUR EARS!' she screamed. 'WE
MUST ROW, OR WE'RE GOING TO FALL!'

She squeezed her hands on either side of her
head, and all the other children imitated her. But
then they couldn't row any more!

'The marzipan!' yelled Holly. 'Put it inside
your ears!'

The children quickly rolled their marzipan

slices into little sausages and stuck them inside
their ears.

(Blastula said, 'Disgusting! We won't even be
able to eat them afterwards!')

(Pepino said, 'Yay! Extra taste!')

The boat was sloping dangerously upwards now, following the stream of water up into the universe …

'ROW!!!!!!!!!' Anna shouted, though no one could hear.

And they started rowing again.

ROW. ROW. ROW. ROW.

ROWROWROWROWROW.

ROWROWROWROWROW.

They rowed so hard that the boat sailed back a bit, laying flat down again on the sea.

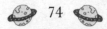 74

But it edged up again …

then was dragged back …

then dropped a bit more

but was dragged back …

and finally …

… there was nothing the children could do any more.

And the boat fell and fell and fell, up and up and up into the dark and empty skies, riding falling waves that gradually dissolved into space.

Chapter Five

The children, pressed against the round windows, watched in horror as the blue-black universe wrapped itself snugly around the drifting boat.

'You people are such useless rowers!' Blastula erupted, taking off her marzipan earplugs.

'Maybe *your drumming* wasn't good enough,' Anna snarled.

'Aren't we going to run out of oxygen soon?' the Tsarina of Marok asked.

'Oh, shucks,' said Pepino. 'I really should have brought a scuba-diving kit. I thought they'd be provided.'

'Scuba-diving kit! Good call, Peps,' said Holly. 'Everyone – get your scuba-diving kits and oxygen bottles. It's the only way to keep breathing.'

'How about *me*?' Pepino cried as the children ran to their cabins.

'You get your space hopper. I'll fill it with some of my oxygen.'

Soon enough, when the boat left the
atmosphere, the space

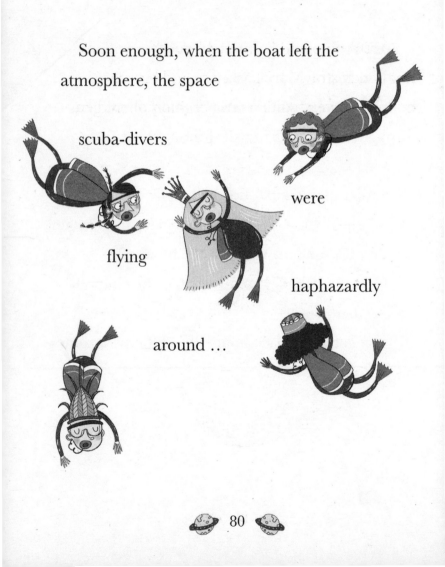

scuba-divers

were

flying

haphazardly

around …

And Pepino had fashioned himself – with a few bendy straws, his fake nose and his space hopper – a very comfortable cushion of oxygen.

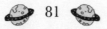

'A*b* I glad I re*bebb*ered to pack that fake *d*ose!' he ~~sniggered~~ sdiggered.

'Wait a second, everyone,' said Anna. 'Where's Hamelin?'

They looked everywhere: no sign of the singer.

'And it's not as if he could be hiding under the furniture,' remarked Ursul, 'since it's flying around.'

'THERE!' Pepino screamed. 'I*d* the sky! He's ru*dd*ing away!'

They all flapped towards the windows of the ship. In the dark blue distance, Hamelin, in full astronaut gear, was indeed running away – or, rather, pedalling away in a space pedal car.

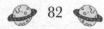

'What a *weirdo*. Well, we're not going to miss him,' Blastula said.

'We need to go get him!' Anna shouted. 'He can't leave us floating into space like this! Find me some rope!'

She swam across the ship as fast as she could and, a few minutes later, she was back with one of the racing cars. She tied a piece of rope to it, knotted the other end to a pillar in the ship and opened a window.

VROOOOOM! She rushed away into the void.

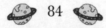

The other children were a little stunned.

'Is she always like that?' Nadya of Marok asked.

'Ofte*d*,' said Pepino. 'She loves showing off.'

'And saving people,' Holly pointed out.

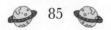

'Well,' Blastula yawned, 'what do we do in the meantime? I'm sure the TVs can't pick up the most interesting channels from here. Are there even kittens left to stroke?'

'Kittens!' Holly jumped. 'We need to make sure the animals are safe. Let's gather all of them and give them some oxygen.'

'Great. You do that while I stand guard!' said Blastula, who crossed her arms and drifted around, showing her (frilly) knickers to everyone.

For the next hour or so, the other children

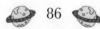

rushed about the boat, floating from room
to room and staircase to staircase to collect
wayward wolverines, cute kittens, purple
puppies, coquettish cockatoos … and – yes –
even the petrifying leopards. *ROAR!*

They fitted them each with space helmets
– balls from the ball pool, or fishbowls for the
bigger ones – linked by a few straws to an oxygen
tank donated by Ursul (who then had to share
Flora's tank; she didn't seem too pleased about
it, but he looked over the moon).

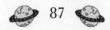

'Well done, everyone!' Holly exclaimed, after squeezing a helmet on to the head of a toothy Tasmanian tiger cub. 'Let's hope the oxygen tanks last long enough for the rescue teams to arrive.'

'*If* they ever arri*be*,' Pepino whispered. 'Oh, do you think they will?'

'*My* rescue team certainly will,' said Blastula. 'As for you, Pepino, I sadly don't think anyone will have the money to come and save you. Plus, I've heard your parents don't care *that* much now that they've got your little brothers. They barely noticed you'd gone to Francia the other week.'

'Stop it, Blastula,' snapped Holly. 'You're making him sad.'

'*D*o, she is*d*'t, I do*d*'t care at all,' said Pepino, but Holly noticed there were tiny little pearls of water flying away from his eyes, and he bounced slowly away on his space hopper.

'Anna's coming back!' Ursul suddenly shouted. 'And she's bringing Hamelin with her!'

'Hello, children,' said Hamelin in his soft and melancholy voice, as Anna dragged him into the ship in his pedal car. 'How have you been?'

'Bored,' said Blastula. 'Why did you bring him back?' she asked Anna. 'He's been nothing but trouble.'

'He was abandoning us!' Anna exclaimed. 'He needs to explain why he's trying to get us lost in space. So? Why?'

'I have my reasons,' said Hamelin. 'If you let me sing you a little song with my mandolin, I'll explain.'

'Oh! Yes! A song!' the children exclaimed.

'Certainly not!' Anna yelled. 'He'll try to entrance us again!

'Just ONE song!' Quetzal implored, seizing the mandolin.

'NO!' Anna retorted, snatching it away.

The debate was suddenly settled, however, when … *ZPLING!* A *harpoon* shot through one of the round windows and broke Hamelin's mandolin in two clean halves.

'MY MANDOLIN!' Hamelin screamed heart-wrenchingly.

And a voice outside, in the cold and dark void, called, 'ATTAAAACK!'

The children looked out of the window, and ...

... spotted the drifting pirate ship.

Chapter Six

At the end of the harpoon was a rope, and at the end of the rope was an alien-looking pirate, or a pirate-looking alien.

That is, he had pirate things, like an eye patch, a parrot on his shoulder and a wooden leg. But he also had alien things, like a great number of eyes that weren't covered by a patch, a great number of shoulders that didn't carry a parrot, and a great number of legs that weren't wooden.

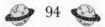

The alien pirate crawled through the window,
yelling, 'Ahoy, space drifters! Surrender or we'll
hang ye from the yardarm!'

'Can you hang people in space?' Holly

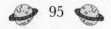

wondered out loud. 'They'd probably just float around being bored.'

'Huh?' the pirate said. 'Quiet, wench! Where be the treasure?'

'You've got a fire-powered wooden leg!' Pepino marvelled. 'I want one!'

'Me too!' said most of the royal children. 'Can I see? Can I see?'

They all gathered around the pirate and pulled on his leg. 'Yaarrh!' he harrumphed. 'What sort of galleon be this? All the shipmen be sprogs!'

'*Royal* sprogs, if you please,' said Blastula. 'Apart from those two dirty little nobodies over there.'

'*Royal* sprogs! Aren't we lucky today!' The pirate rubbed his hands. 'And who be the bigger lad o'er there?'

'Only a musician whose instrument and will to live you've just broken,' cried Hamelin.

'Arrrh! Sorry, me lad. We'll find you another o' both o' those things in the next galley!'

And he slapped Hamelin's back, sending him flying straight to the other side of the room.

'So where be that treasure, then?' he asked, looking around. 'All I see's sprogs and animals with straws and air tanks.'

'And *where be* your other pirate friends?' Anna asked. 'Who's in that gigantic ship?'

'Well, me beauty, all me buccaneers. If ye let me take ye thar as prisoners, I'll show ye. They be a *bit strange*, but good mateys.'

'What, stranger than *you*?' Blastula gasped.

'Let's by all means stay here, then.'

'Oh, no, please make us prisoners!' the other children implored.

Pepino was jumping up and down with joy, which in space meant jumping from wall to wall to wall in all different directions. 'It sounds like the most fun anyone could *ever* have,' he said.

'That ship looks very dirty,' Blastula remarked. 'Do you even have running water?'

'Nay, but look at the air bubble! I built it meself! Ye can breathe normally on thar!'

'Very impressive,' Anna mulled, looking at the ship. 'I do think we should go. It's tiring carrying these scuba-diving kits around, and we might have a chance of survival there until we're rescued. And we can try to get the truth out of Hamelin … OK, take us prisoners, Mr … Mr … ?'

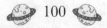

'Me name's Twig-Leg Zig, and the name o' that beauty over thar's the *Void Vagrant*! Nay, let's not bother with the prisoner business. Ye look like a bunch o' good buckos. Ready to work for the glory o' the *Vagrant*?'

'YES!' yelled all the children.

'Certainly not,' piped Hamelin.

'Work *again*?' sighed Anna, Holly and Pepino. 'How much work are we talking about here? We were sort of hoping this would be a holiday, before it was ruined for us.'

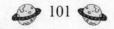

'Ye'll have to attack all the galleys we meet,' said Zig. 'Especially if they be comin' from Earth, with good treasures.'

'How often is that?'

'Ye be the first one in forty-eight years.'

'Oh. That sounds manageable. What else will we have to do?'

'Rid the keel o' space barnacles, make salmagundi for dinner, repair the sails and stand atop the crow's nest, looking through the spyglass for the man an' the white bird.'

'The *what*?'

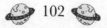

But Zig was tired of giving details. 'Avast!' he shouted. 'Follow me now or ye'll be made t'walk the plank!'

'Can you walk the plank in space?' Holly wondered. 'Wouldn't you just fall off into the sky and be bored?'

'AVAST, WENCH!' Twig-Leg Zig shouted.

So he and the children left the drifting Holy Moly Holiday ship and flew across the big empty skies towards the *Void Vagrant*, carrying, in rescue boats, the animals, the tied-up Pip Hamelin, one racing car and one pedal car.

Chapter Seven

The other buccaneers were certainly good buckos, and also aliens; Twig-Leg Zig had picked them up from passing comets and UFOs. They worked alongside the royal children, which was lucky because Twig-Leg Zig hadn't joked when he'd told them about the jobs to do on the *Void Vagrant*.

Holly was on barnacle duty. Ridding the keel

of space barnacles was no small task. Space barnacles are a particularly gluey and prickly kind of extraterrestrial parasite. They are characterised by three tricky things: a super-sticky sucker, angry burning little eyes and sharpish shards on the shell.

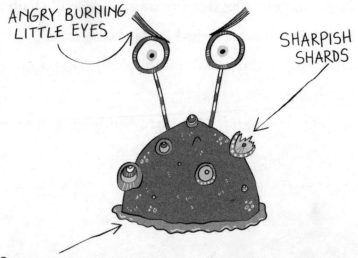

ANGRY BURNING LITTLE EYES

SHARPISH SHARDS

SUPER-STICKY SUCKER

To scrape them off the keel of the ship – as you float around, whooshing through space – you have to use a razor-sharp knife, and as they angrily loosen their grip, their little eyes shoot hot laser beams …

But once they're off and away into the dark and empty void, they turn into peacock-coloured hummingbird-sized flying creatures, and they go looking for other celestial bodies to stick to.

'They're so beautiful!' Holly sighed every time a space barnacle flew away. 'I wish I could keep one on my shoulder as a pet.'

'Nay, ye don't!' growled Zig one day, when he was within earshot. 'Nasty little beasties, those be! They'd suck ya soul through ya skin and burn anybody that came near!'

Pepino was in the kitchens on salmagundi duty, and after a week he began to complain:

'I *still* don't know what the recipe's supposed to be … nor what ingredients I'm using!'

'Just mix them all together, me lad! It's not complicated!'

 108

The ingredients were gathered from a large net that always hung behind the ship as it drifted. It caught small fry (tiny shrimp-like aliens, mini space-eels, sky algae) and sometimes, when they were very lucky, a warm meteorite with a whole unknown ecosystem on it.

'Do you think I can use this fruit-like thing?' Pepino asked. 'How do I know it's not toxic?'

'Test it on Blastula first,' Anna whispered.

Blastula had landed the laziest job on the ship, as she had proven too useless and squeamish to do any of the others. It involved sitting atop the mizzen mast, with a spyglass made of diamonds and melted metals Zig had found on passing comets. Her job was to peer at the dark and empty skies in the hope of spotting 'the man an' the white bird'.

'The man an' the white bird' was Twig-Leg

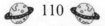

Zig's favourite story, and his most important mission in his space-pirate life.

'It all happened a few years ago,' he'd told them on the very first night, as all the children had gathered in the fo'c'sle, where their hammocks hung. 'Or maybe more than a few years. What with the night all the time, where be certainty about anything? I'm flying down the futtock of the *Vagrant*, to repair the broken bits, and I look into the sky and suddenly I see him. I see him like I see ye now. I see *the man an' the white bird!*'

Zig let a long and mysterious silence settle.

'They be flying fast and sure, like they know where to go. An' I scream at them, "Are ye a god? Or an angel?" And the man-angel looks at me sadly and waves his hand. I say, "Ahoy! Angel!" and watch them go … And then I never see them again.'

'Never?' Pepino whispered.

'Never. Every day, I go up to the crow's nest and I watch the sky with the spyglass. I see nay man and bird, nay ever.'

He turned to Blastula. 'But with those eyes o' yours, ye'll see him, I know it! He be coming back and bringing joy an' happiness to all of us!'

Since then, Blastula had half-heartedly 'worked' to find the man and the bird. At every meal she complained and groaned, 'That silly dirty pirate had a hallucination all those years ago and now *we* have to waste our time looking for something that doesn't exist!'

'At least you're not scraping barnacles off the keel of the ship,' Anna murmured. 'Think of my sister.'

'She's a commoner – that's what they're for,' Blastula retorted. '*I'm* more sad for my poor *royal* friends who are slaving away down this mast, keeping the boat going, when they should be twirling around at balls and learning to wave at peasants while simultaneously smiling!'

The other royal children, though, didn't seem too bothered. If anything, they *loved* slaving away on the pirate ship with the other buccaneers.

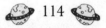

The tsarina, Nadya of Marok, worked with Arak, a seamstress from planet Vega, repairing the sails of the *Void Vagrant*.

A team of ten dukelings, emperorlets and princesses checked the nets and caught drifting

meteorites with the help of
Big-Paw Pam, who'd been a
Plutonian baseball champion
in his youth.

Countess Graupel of Alaskold, who was used
to cold temperatures, harvested ice from passing
comets and gave it to the frazzling-hot Sun-born
twin brothers, Sol and Brul, to melt into water.

Three of the other children
were in charge of the now
rather huge menagerie on
the ship, and the animals
were having a bit too much
fun flying around.

Meanwhile, Anna had the job of looking after their only prisoner: Hamelin.

Ten times a day, she asked him, 'Tell me the truth. *Why* did you try to lose us into the sky?'

But Hamelin was *not* cooperating.

'I'll tell you only if you fix my mandolin,' he grumbled in reply, ten times a day. 'You could use barnacle glue and ask Mrs Arak for help with the strings.'

'If I do that, you'll just try to entrance us again by singing another song.'

He shrugged. 'It's up to you …'

118

And then sometimes he'd smile slyly and say, 'It's a *good* story, though …'

'I don't care about your silly story,' Anna said.

But she did feel curious to know what the story was …

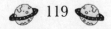

Chapter Eight

'**A**rrr!!!' yelled Twig-Leg Zig one sort-of-morning. 'Show a leg, sprogs! Planet in sight! All hands on deck for mooring!'

'Thank *goodness*,' Blastula said with a yawn from the top of the crow's nest. 'If that pirate stops going further and further into the sky, we might have a chance to be rescued one day. I can't *wait* to take a break from you smelly people!'

And she threw the spyglass to – or rather *at* – Anna, narrowly missing her head. Anna pocketed it.

The *Void Vagrant* was indeed drifting towards a tiny planet, green and fluffy like a plush ball. They slowly entered its atmosphere and threw the anchor down into a large forest. Each tree was like a giant lollipop of moss, ruffled by bird-like animals.

'Are you *sure* it's wise to come here?' asked Nadya. 'How do you know we won't get eaten by the alien wild beasts?'

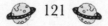

'Slides down!' roared Zig, ignoring her entirely.

'Let's take Hamelin with us,' said Anna. 'It's safer. Goodness knows what he'd do here on his own.'

'And we can always feed him to the alien wild beasts, if there are any,' said Nadya.

Hamelin shrugged. Anna tied him to his flying pedal car, which she tied to herself, and they all whooshed down the corkscrew slides to the ground.

'Have you been here before?' Holly asked Arak and Big-Paw Pam.

Arak hissed a Veganese 'No': '*Hksz.*'

Big-Paw Pam, who spoke only with his hands, mimed the winds and the ship, then shrugged: *the sky-winds take the ship wherever they like; we can't decide.*

'Where be the booty?' Zig yelled, jumping amid the velvet-soft herbs and trees. 'Coffers full o' doubloons, all kinds o' loot from interplanetary pillages! Come on, sprogs – look out for treasure!'

'I wish he wouldn't do that – it's so *embarrassing*,' said Holly. Big-Paw Pam nodded and squashed a red fruit all over his face to express the fact that he was blushing with shame.

'Oh, look,' said Pepino as they walked across the jungle. 'Potato-type things. Maybe I could use them for my next salmagundi.'

They stopped to look at the round white things clustered on a purple leaf.

'They're moving a bit,' Anna noted. 'Are you sure they're not eggs?'

Indeed, the potato-type things were clicking

and shaking, and suddenly – *CRACK!* – they began to snap. Four ferocious-looking feral *things* forced their way out of the frozen shells, flashed their fangs and flapped their five little wings.

A few seconds later, they'd flown off into the forest.

'Phew,' said Pepino. 'It's very difficult to ensure food safety in the dark and empty skies.'

'It's not food you should worry about,' chimed Hamelin.

Anna turned to him. 'What do you mean?'

'Oh, nothing,' said Hamelin, leaning back into his pedal car.

'You are *so* annoying!' she growled.

'Look,' Holly said, 'there are four suns on this planet!'

They watched them for a while.

'And more of these flying things,' said Quetzal.

'A lot of them,' Pepino confirmed. 'At least …
five or six. Or even … ten … twenty … I can't really
count them. They're flying together in swarms!'

'Yes, that's what they do,' said Hamelin dreamily.

Anna turned to him.

'What do you mean, "That's what they do"?'

'Did I say that?' Hamelin asked. 'Oh, nothing.'

'HAMELIN!' Anna shouted. 'Have you seen these things before?'

He yawned. 'I might be mistaken. It's been a long time.'

'They're coming towards us,' Holly said. 'They're … I mean, I can't tell if they're friendly or … Zig? Zig, can you … Can you have a look

129

at those, up there, and tell us if you think they're nice?'

Twig-Leg Zig rolled his ten eyes (minus the one behind the eye patch) up into the sky.

'I have no idea, me lass, but all I can tell ye is that those creatures thar are th'ugliest I've seen in a while! Like a cross between a rat an' butterfly, those things are!'

Holly looked at Anna.

'Rat and butterfly,' she murmured.

'What about it?' asked Anna, raising her eyebrows.

'Doesn't that remind you of something?'

Hamelin, behind them, sniggered.

'She's got a good memory, that one ...'

And Anna suddenly remembered.

'The *Things*?' she whispered. 'The *Things* from the song? They're ... they're real?'

'RUN!!!' Holly yelled. 'EVERYONE, RUN!!!'

And as the Things dived down, the children and the alien pirates ran and ran and ran to find a place to hide.

They soon came to a large rock and had to split into two groups: to the left went Anna, Hamelin, Blastula and the pirates; to the right went Holly, Pepino and the other children.

A few minutes later, Anna and her group

found a burrow to – *pop!* – leap into. And a few seconds later, Holly, Pepino and their group found a cave to – *whoosh!* – run into.

They could hear the angry buzz of Things above their heads.

Then silence.

'OK,' said Anna to Hamelin. 'Now explain to us what happened. How do you know about these Things?'

'I'll explain when you've fixed my mandolin.'

'*Right!*' Anna exploded. 'We'll fix your *stupid* mandolin!'

 133

She squeezed the two pieces out of the pedal car and, in the bright light of Sol and Brul, began to repair the instrument.

First Twig-Leg Zig scraped a barnacle off the back of the pedal car. They squeezed its gluey dribble on to the body of the mandolin.

Then Arak carefully knitted back the strings.

Finally, they untied Hamelin and gave him the mandolin.

Tzing! Tzing!

'It's not very well tuned,' he said reproachfully.

'Then tune it!' Anna groaned.

From *tzing!* to *gling!* to *drling, drling!* the mandolin found its enchanting tunes again.

And Hamelin began to sing:

> *Remember, friends, our brave young player*
> *Who had led all the Things away?*
> *He went back home, and voiced his prayer:*

'I did it – now, in place of pay,
As we agreed, let me espouse
The princess of this Royal House
For I love her, and she loves me.'
But the King said, 'Alas, my lad,
No one knows where your love may be;
She's disappeared; we're very sad.'

(Hearing this, the solar brothers shed some tears,
which sizzled over their burning bodies and
evaporated in puffs of steam.)

The boy did not believe a word
Of the terrible thing he'd heard
He knew the King had surely lied:
His own daughter he'd hid away
So she could never be his bride.
In anger and in disarray
The singer made the deathly plan
To hurt the royals where they'd hurt him.
Just like the toxic Things before them
He'd lead away the royal children.
And thus he started plottin', plottin'

A cunning plan to send away
The princesses and princes rotten
On a long, one-way Holiday.

Hamelin stopped there. 'Do you want me to continue?'

Shaken from their reverie, Anna, Zig, Pam, the solar brothers and Arak jumped.

'Wait a minute,' Anna stuttered. 'Is this the truth? *You* were the musician they asked to lead the Things away from Earth?'

'You guessed! How clever of you.' Hamelin smirked.

'You did the same thing to them as you did to us – led them away to the Southern Edge of the Earth in a boat?'

'That was the suggestion of the royals, yes.'

'And then you escaped, as you planned to escape from our boat?'

'Worked better the first time around,' Hamelin acknowledged.

'And then they refused to give their daughter to you? And that's why you lost us into the sky? For *revenge*?'

'Of course,' said Hamelin sadly. 'Love and revenge: is there anything else in the world?'

Bzzz … bzzz … went a noise above their heads.

And they realised the Things were burrowing through the ground to reach them.

'Aye!' Zig exclaimed. 'Thar's other things than love an' revenge! Thar's BATTLE! BATTLE against the darn Things!'

So they all braced themselves for it – braced themselves for the *Things* coming at them.

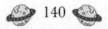

Chapter Nine

Meanwhile, Holly, Pepino and the other children had managed to push a large stone across the opening of their cave to prevent the Things from flying in. In the dark, they walked down a sloped corridor, which led towards an underground cavern, bathed in the strange, white, fluorescent light of the liana vines that hung from the ceiling.

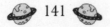

'What is this place?' Ursul marvelled. 'It's almost like a weird palace.'

'What are those *plants*?' Nadya asked, fiddling with one of the glistening lianas. 'They look like bogeys. And they're rubbery like chewing gum.'

'It smells of bubbly soup cooking,' said Pepino. 'I'm hungry.'

'It *can't* smell of bubbly soup,' Blastula
snapped. 'It's an alien planet peopled only with
dangerous flying Things.'

'It *does* smell of bubbly soup, though,' Holly
remarked. 'It even *sounds* like soup is gently
bubbling on a stove.'

And it was.

In a corner of the cave, in the milky light of
the mosses, was a woman attending to a bubbly
pot on a small fire.

The young woman stood up when she saw the children. She wore a shredded white dress and had large black eyes like the skies they'd been crossing for days.

'You're a human,' whispered Holly.

'Yes,' said the lady. 'Hello.' She seemed a little bit distracted. 'I haven't spoken to humans for a while.'

'How long?'

'Many years. Soup?'

They all nodded, and the lady poured soup for each of them in hollow stones.

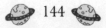

'Who are you?' Pepino asked. 'How did you get here?'

'My name is – or was – Princess Fandorin of Rossia. I fell into the sky on a boat,' she said.

'Just like us!' Blastula exclaimed. 'Were you also going on a Holy Moly Holiday?'

'No,' said the lady, 'I was trying to get married. But my future husband let the boat I was in fall into the sky, and he escaped.'

'What? He left you to drift away into space?'

'Yes,' said the lady sadly. 'Though, to be honest, he didn't know I was *on* the boat.

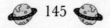

You see, I …'

She turned towards the entrance to the cave.
'I can hear Things buzzing. Did you roll the
stone across the opening?'

'Sort of,' said Blastula. 'It was a bit heavy, so I
couldn't be bothered to roll it all the way.'

'*Great*,' Holly growled. 'Does it mean they're
going to come in?'

'Yes,' said Fandorin. 'Quick, grab some of those lianas and use them as slingshots to fire pebbles at them. That's the only language they understand.'

A few seconds later, a swarm of Things invaded the cave, buzzing furiously. The children pulled on the rubbery, bogey-like lianas, which were elastic enough to be used as slingshots – and the terrible battle began.

SLING! One well-aimed shot from Fandorin, who seemed to be used to the exercise, hit a Thing right on its angry little nose.

PING! Holly's pebble hit a Thing's wing, and it screeched with annoyance, flying back.

PZING! PZING! Blastula's and Pepino's shots hit the exact same Thing at the same time.

'Hey!' Pepino yelled. 'Well done, us!'

 And they exchanged a tiny high five.

Soon they realised this was the way to go: hitting one

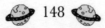

Thing with two stones.

'This one over here, with the purple antennae!' shouted Pepino.

PZING! PZING!

The second time Pepino and Blastula high-fived, it was a normal high five.

The third time and afterwards, it

 was a strong, hearty, roaring sort of high five!

And after they'd scared away the last enormous

squeaky Thing by shooting many stones at him,
something really quite awkward happened. They
hugged.

'Urgh!' said Pepino.
'That's disgusting!'

'The most yucky
thing in the world,'
Blastula agreed. 'And
I'm sure you crinkled
my dress.'

'But well done
anyway,' said Pepino.

'Yes, well done anyway,' whispered Blastula.

'Soup?' asked Fandorin, as if nothing out of the ordinary had happened.

'No,' said Holly. 'We need to leave this cave and find Anna, Zig and the others. They might be in danger.'

'*You* might need to leave,' Blastula said, 'but I'm staying here and having soup. I've done enough fighting for today.'

'Suit yourself,' Holly groaned. 'I'm going, and Pepino is too.'

'Am I?' Pepino asked.

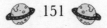 151

'Of course you are! It's Anna! She's somewhere on this dangerous planet with only Zig, Arak, Pam and the brothers to help her – it's not as if she could count on Hamelin!'

CLANK! The wooden ladle of soup that Princess Fandorin was holding fell on the stone floor of the cave. 'Who?' she asked faintly.

'Pip Hamelin. The man who took us on this fake holiday and lost us all in space. Come on, Pepino, let's go!'

'We're *all* going,' Fandorin stated calmly. 'Take your slingshots and some pebbles.'

'I HATE this holiday,' Blastula grumbled, 'and I'll have you all put in the stocks when we're back on Earth.'

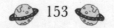

Chapter Ten

In the burrow, Anna, Arak, Zig, Pam and the solar brothers were desperately trying to fight the Things.

They were *fairly* successful. Sol and Brul couldn't be stung, since their bodies were made mostly of fire. *Grrrzz!* They burnt the Things by flicking their fingers.

Twig-Leg Zig had developed a kind of kung-fu kick with his wooden leg – *PAF!* – and Arak

was trapping the Things in her webs.

Anna, meanwhile, was using Hamelin's mandolin to hit the Things.

'If you'll only let me have it …' Hamelin muttered.

'Shut up, Hamelin! This is battle time, not music time!'

'But I —'

'You've given us enough trouble!'

Eventually, Hamelin cleared his throat. 'Holy moly! Anna, my dear, you are sometimes remarkably obtuse. Remember the story I just told you? Wasn't there a part about the musician being the only person able to entrance the Things?'

Anna stopped. 'Oh,' she said. 'Hmm. Right.'

'May I?'

She handed the mandolin to Hamelin and he began to strum the strings.

And the soft, watery, angelic melody, resonating throughout the burrow and beyond,

 156

made the Things suddenly slow down and …
dance.

They were dancing, swirling, twirling around,
completely enchanted by Hamelin's mellow
tunes.

Anna, Arak, Zig and the brothers, just as entranced, emerged from the burrow, following Hamelin and his sweet music. Around them, the jungle was peaceful, almost as if the trees themselves were gently swaying to the mandolin's melodies. And the Things, pacified, drifted around them in mid-air …

'ANNA!' shouted a voice from the bushes. 'HOLLY! PEPINO!'

The three children ran into each other's arms. 'We fought the Things with slingshots!' Pepino yelled.

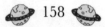

'We're fighting them with music,' Anna replied. 'Well, Hamelin is. First useful thing he's ever done.'

'We found a cave,' Holly said. 'And inside there was a princess.'

'*Another one?* Is there one place in this universe that doesn't have royals?'

One by one, the other children emerged from the jungle, dazzled by Hamelin's music and by the hypnotising dance of the Things.

'It's Hamelin!' Blastula sighed. 'He's controlling the Things!'

All the children sat down around Hamelin as he sang:

> *And so it is that in this jungle,*
> *Forever sad, forever single,*
> *Without his one true love and friend,*
> *The singer's story must now end,*
> *Playing his mournful mandolin,*
> *Missing his lovely ...*

'Fandorin,' said a calm and lovely voice.

The children and the pirates jumped.

Fandorin, in her white dress, had just appeared from behind a tree.

'Fandorin!' Hamelin repeated, staring wide-eyed at the young woman.

'I knew we had to be reunited somehow,' she murmured.

'How did you … how did you …'

'How did I get here? I was on the boat the whole time. I knew my parents wouldn't let me marry you when you got back, so I sneaked into the ship and hid in a rescue boat so we could elope once you'd sent the Things into space.

But I didn't get out in time. You'd already left the ship, and it was drifting away into the empty skies … I stayed on it for weeks and weeks, until it landed on this planet. I've been living here alone with all the Things.'

The two young people drew closer to one another, and Hamelin knelt down to take his beloved's hand. 'Oh, Fandorin! Why didn't you say you were on the ship?'

'I didn't want to distract you from your mission! You had to keep playing.'

'But if I'd known …'

'It's OK,' she said. 'We can get married now. I'm wearing a white dress.'

'I will marry you in three seconds if you let me,' he whispered.

'We need someone to perform the wedding,' Fandorin said.

Big-Paw Pam got up first. He made a heart with his hands, then pointed at the two lovers – and finally pushed them gently together into a kiss.

'I think that means: "I declare you husband and wife!"' said Anna.

'HURRAH!' everyone cheered.

'Let's never go back to Earth,' said Hamelin to Fandorin.

'Why don't ye come with us on the *Vagrant*?' Twig-Leg Zig asked. 'We always need extra pairs o' hands. And you might make us some more sprogs to help!'

'Sounds great,' said Holly, 'but you might want to start playing the mandolin again, Hamelin. The Things are waking up from their

daze, and they look like they want to sting us again.'

Hamelin sighed, picking up his instrument, and as he played he led them all through the jungle to Fandorin's cave.

Chapter Eleven

'Ahoy, me sprogs!' Twig-Leg Zig shouted the next morning when they all woke up in the cave where they'd spent the night. 'All hands on deck! Time t'work! We found nay booty on this isle.'

'You mean we're going back in the boat?' yawned Ursul of Quebecque. 'Why?'

'A pirate never abandons a ship for the lures o' the land!' Zig growled.

'Now wait a minute,' said Blastula. 'You can take your dusty boat and drift away at some point, but *I'm* staying here and waiting for Mummy and Daddy to come and pick us up. And we're keeping Hamelin in the meantime to protect us from the Things. He owes us *at least* that.'

'I agree with Blastula,' said Ursul. 'We can't keep floating from planet to planet.' Protected from the Things by Hamelin's music, they all left the cave and looked around for ways to make themselves known.

'OK, everyone,' Blastula shouted, 'let's build

a giant flag on this planet with a drawing of my head on it, so they can see where we are.'

'Great, let me do the drawing,' said Anna, doodling something in the sand that resembled a pig with a crown on its head.

The children chuckled. Blastula glared at Anna. 'You can be sure your mum and dad won't be looking for *you*. I'm sure *your* dad doesn't even have a rocket! He's probably a smelly, dirty little man doing a boring job.'

'*No*,' said Holly, taking the family picture out of her pocket. 'He's none of that. He's *that man*. And he's gone away forever. Happy?'

'That was mean of you!' said Pepino to Blastula. 'We've had enough of your nastiness. Say sorry.'

Blastula was embarrassed. Everywhere she looked, be it towards Anna, Holly, Pepino,

Big-Paw Pam or even her best friends Ursul, Nadya and Constantino, or worse – Arak's eighteen reproachful eyes – she only saw annoyance.

'I'm sorry,' she muttered. 'I'm sorry your dad isn't able to come and pick you up. I mean, I'm sorry he's disappeared and all that. And I'm sure he wasn't smelly or dirty.'

Anna and Holly smiled, and for the first time Blastula smiled back.

'And who be looking for the angel an' the bird if ye all leave me?' Twig-Leg Zig groaned. 'I need someone up thar on the mast!'

'Oh, shut up, Zig,' said Anna. 'You can ask Fandorin or Hamelin to do it. Here, I've got your spyglass – you can even look at the skies from here in the meantime. Let me see … No! No angel and no bird. Nothing at all that's interes–'

She froze.

'What be it?' Zig asked. '*What be it?*'

Anna couldn't believe what she was seeing.

Blastula grabbed the spyglass and looked through it too. 'I KNEW IT!' she yelled, seeing a rocket with her name emblazoned on its side. 'They're coming to look for me! They're coming, they're coming, they're *coming*!'

She danced with joy and looked again. 'Oh! Ursul! There's one for you too! And … yes, I can see one with your name on it, Quetzal!'

All the children took turns to look into the

spyglass, shrieking with joy.

'Arrrr,' Zig groaned. 'They be a bit far from away still, but in two or three days there'll be here …'

It was Pepino's turn to take the spyglass. He stared and stared and stared into it.

'Oh! I can see the rocket with my name on it!' he exclaimed. 'Oh no, wait. That says "Petunia" … Maybe it's hidden behind another rocket … Maybe …'

All the royal children threw awkward glances at him, and even Blastula didn't dare say anything.

Anna wrapped her arm around Pepino's shoulder. 'Don't worry, Peps,' she said. 'I'm sure

your parents will send a rescue mission too.'

'But I think we spent all our rescue mission budget for this year on new toboggans,' Pepino whispered.

'You three can come with me in my rocket,' said Nadya. 'We'll have enough space. It's a huge rocket. It's got a tennis court in it.'

'Thank you,' said Holly. 'See, Peps? We'll go back to Earth anyway.'

Pepino nodded and sniffed.

'Well,' Blastula said, coughing, 'shall we get started on that giant flag, then?'

So over the next two days, they found the tallest tree on the planet, made it even taller by strapping another tall tree to it, and Arak knitted the most gigantic triangle of fabric she could.

Some of the children made paints from fruits, flowers and mashed-up stones. And the other children used them to paint the giant flag.

And sometimes their own faces by accident.

A thousand times a day, they looked into the spyglass to check the progress of the rockets …

And still there was none for Pepino.

Then the next evening, they lifted up the flag over the little planet.

The rockets were getting closer and closer.
'They'll be here tomorrow!' Blastula exclaimed,
looking into the spyglass. 'Oh, I hope Mummy
and Daddy have brought my twelve fox terriers!
Or my six favourites, at least.'

That night, they had a leaving party in the
cave. They danced, ate and told stories, and
imagined what it would be like to go back to
Earth.

'I can't wait to eat popcorn again!' Ursul said.
'But I *can* wait to start doing homework again.
What month is it? Probably almost September.

Time to go back to school.'

'Zig,' said Quetzal, 'are you sure you don't want to come to Earth? It's great, you know! And you can ride in my rocket if you want! I'm sure my parents won't mind. If you take a shower first, that is.'

Zig fidgeted uncomfortably. 'That's very nice of ye, me lad, but I'm a space pirate, not an Earth pirate. I like the taste o' the falling stardust.'

He held one of Big-Paw Pam's huge fingers in one hand and one of Arak's legs with the

other, winked to the solar twins and said to the children: 'Don't be sad, sprogs! I'll miss ye all, but the booty I have t'find is up thar, nay down thar.'

The next morning, all the rockets were visible without even looking through the spyglass. (Flora, or Flopsy-Diddle-Doo, was not too happy that her nickname had been made so public on the side of her rocket.)

All the children collected their belongings and stood on the main deck of the pirate ship, from which Twig-Leg Zig had put out a long plank into the sky. The rockets were parked one next to the other, waiting to pick up the children.

Blastula was the first to walk the plank. 'Bye-bye, everyone! It was a fun holiday! I hope we find another summer camp we can all go to next year!'

Then it was Ursul's turn. 'Send postcards!' he shouted to everyone. 'I'll miss you!'

And one by one the children hugged their

friends, Twig-Leg Zig, Arak and Big-Paw Pam
(but not the solar brothers, who weren't very
huggable), and walked down the plank to board
the rockets waiting for them.

'I'll take you back to Earth,' said Nadya of
Marok to Anna and Holly when it was her turn.
'Where's Pepino?'

'No idea,' Anna said. 'Have you seen him
anywhere?'

'Well …' Nadya blushed. 'This morning,
when we were packing our stuff, I was talking
to Blastula and Quetzal, and … we didn't mean

 183

to be rude … we just said something like, "Isn't it weird that Pepino's parents haven't sent a rocket?" And Blastula said, "Poor Pepino! He really isn't loved, is he? I used to dislike him, but now all I feel is pity." And we all agreed and said much the same thing.'

'That's not very nice,' said Holly. 'But why are you telling us this?'

The Tsarina of Marok bit her lip. 'Well, when I left the fo'c'sle, I noticed Pepino had been standing in the corner the whole time. He must have overheard our conversation.'

Anna and Holly stared at each other, horrified.

Twig-Leg Zig, behind them, said, 'Look into the spyglass, me lassies! Who be up thar in Hamelin's pedal car, flying away as fast as he can? Pepino!'

Anna and Holly grabbed the spyglass and their blood curdled.

'Oh, no! Where's he *going*?'

'I need to go. My rocket's here,' said Nadya. 'Are you coming or not?'

Anna and Holly looked at each other and sighed. 'No,' said Holly. 'We need to get Pepino. He's our friend.'

The Tsarina of Marok shrugged and said goodbye to everyone. A few seconds later, she'd gone into the rocket, the rocket door had clicked shut and she was gone.

'Quick,' said Anna. 'The racing car – and our scuba-diving kits. Zig, we're leaving – we need

 186

to catch Pepino.'

'That's the right attitude, me sprogs,' said Zig. 'I'll be sorry t'see ye leave, but ye can't let a bucko get lost in the sky like that. Take me spyglass – I'll make another one.'

Anna and Holly hugged the buccaneers of the *Void Vagrant*, and Zig even shed a few tears. Anna too, perhaps, and Holly certainly. As for Arak, it was very obvious, since there were so many eyes on her.

And then they got into the racing car and took off.

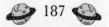

Chapter Twelve

Because Anna and Holly were in a racing car and Pepino was pedalling on his own – and because Pepino wasn't especially good at pedalling – they caught up with him pretty quickly.

'Pepino! What are you *doing*?' Holly shouted. 'All the rockets have gone!'

'Why haven't you left?' the prince replied. 'You should have!'

'We weren't going to leave you alone! Where do you think you're going?'

'I don't care. Anywhere. I want to find a nice little planet just for myself, where I can be all on my own.'

'That sounds sad,' said Anna.

'I *am* sad,' said Pepino.

'Well, we're not leaving you alone,' Holly stated. 'We'll come to your little planet with you.'

And they drove in silence for what felt an eternity in the very empty and very dark skies. They were so far from any suns now that it was mostly dark, and quite cold.

'There's a little planet over there,' said Anna after a while, looking into the spyglass. 'It's very, very little.'

'Sounds perfect,' said Pepino grumpily.

The planet was indeed very, very little.

It was also, it turned out, already occupied, for there was a tiny cottage there, with a large bird perched upon the roof.

'Looks like a bird's living here,' said Holly.

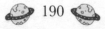 190

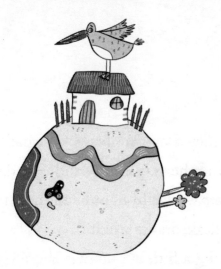

'Shall we see if we can find anything to eat or drink in that cottage before we leave again?'

'It's such a small planet,' Anna mulled. 'Will we even have enough space to land?'

They did, just about. There was barely anywhere to stand. They took off their scuba-diving and breathing kits – the air was quite breathable, and smelt familiar.

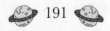

'I feel like I've seen this bird before,' said Holly. 'Shall we knock on the door?'

'I guess we might as well,' said Anna. 'I hope it's not an ogre or a witch.'

They knocked, but no one came to the door.

So they pushed it open and looked inside.

'I feel like I've seen this fellow before,' said

Pepino, looking at a man asleep in the bed. 'Have you?'

Anna and Holly didn't reply. They just stared at the sleeping man.

'Oh, I know,' said Pepino. 'I know where I've seen him … It was a few days ago. When you showed that picture to Blastula. That picture of …'

Pepino stopped. 'Oh, Anna! Holly! This is your … It's your …'

'*Daddy*,' Holly and Anna whispered at the same time.

Very slowly, they walked to the bed. The man was sleeping calmly and snoring a little bit.

Holly and Anna bent down ... and kissed his cheek.

What happened next can't be explained very well with words ...

And then there were too many words …

And very, very, very many kisses.

Many kisses and stories for the next few days and nights.

Chapter Thirteen

One sort-of-morning, suddenly, they heard a sound outside the door of the cottage.

A sound like the huffs and puffs of someone pedalling hard when they're *not very good at exercising* …

… and a voice harrumphing, 'I *really* wish we hadn't spent the rescue mission budget on those new toboggans.'

'I know, my dear,' said a second familiar voice. 'You keep saying this. Maybe the people on this planet will be able to help. *Ahem, ahem,* excuse me? Is *anyone* home? We're looking for a tiny sort of prince, with cute little cheeks and messy hair. And two girls: a bossy one and another one with glasses, both very cute too.'

Pepino stared at Anna, then Holly, as if he couldn't believe what he was hearing.

And then he was out of the house in a flash. The girls and their dad followed him.

'MUMMY!!!!!!!!! DADDY!!!!!!!!!!!!!!!!!'

'Oh, Pepino, darling!' the King and Queen of
Britland exclaimed, hovering beside the cottage
in their pedal rocket. 'We've been looking for you
all over the entire *universe*!'

'Have you *really*?' Pepino marvelled, jumping into his parents' arms.

'It was quite slow,' said King Steve, 'because we had to build this rocket from scratch, and then pedal through space for weeks. I must say, your mum's become devilishly good at pedalling. She should take part in the Tour de Francia.'

'Oh, Mummy, Daddy,' Pepino whispered, hugging his parents. 'I was so worried you didn't care I'd gone!'

'Didn't *care*?' Queen Sheila laughed. 'There wasn't a *second* when we didn't miss our grumpy,

 200

ice-cream-covered, chubby, funny, lovely little prince!'

'We even brought you ice cream,' said King Steve, 'but it's a tad melted, and, erm, I ate a bit of it.'

But it was the most delicious ice cream Pepino had ever eaten.

'Where are the Berties?' Anna asked.

'Being babysat by Nestor. I hope he doesn't mind that we've been gone for much longer than we said.'

'And I hope King Alaspooryorick hasn't heard you were away,' laughed Holly.

'Shall we give you a ride home, then?' the King and Queen asked Holly, Anna and their dad. 'It'll be quicker with all of us pedalling.'

'I can't wait to stretch my legs a little bit,' said Holly and Anna's dad. 'It's been a while since the last time I was able to walk more than a few steps.'

So they all got into the pedal rocket – even the pelican, who, it turned out, could pedal quite well when he put his mind to it.

 202

And they pedalled and they pedalled in the dark and empty skies, passing by planets, UFOs and flotsam from the Earth and other places, passing by the pirate spaceship too …

And through his spyglass, Twig-Leg Zig watched them go by and he smiled, saying, 'Arrr! The man an' the bird! Thar he is. I knew something good would come o' that in the end. I knew it was a special man an' a special bird. I *knew* it.'

And they pedalled and pedalled until the
Earth was in sight …

… and then through the Earth's
atmosphere …

… and straight to Britland …

… and down to the small
seaside village of Doverport, which thankfully
hadn't been invaded at all (though Nestor looked
a tiny bit tired).

And when they landed it was already
September – in fact, the school bell was *just
ringing* for the first morning class!

'Come to school with us, Pepino,' said Anna.
'You'll have much more fun than with your
private tutor at the castle!'

'Yes,' said the King and Queen, 'it's probably
a good idea. You go off to school and make new
friends and learn new things.'

'YIPPEE!!!!'

Pepino was so happy he tried to do a triple
somersault, forgetting he wasn't in space any

more, and landed on his head.

But Anna wasn't happy.

In fact, she was quite *grumpy*.

'School!' she grumbled. '*School!* Already? We've *barely had a holiday*!'

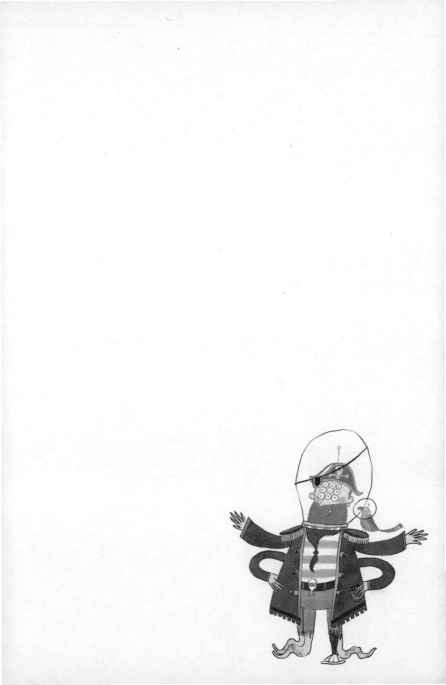

FIND OUT WHERE IT ALL BEGAN
Join Holly, Anna and Pepino
on their first adventure

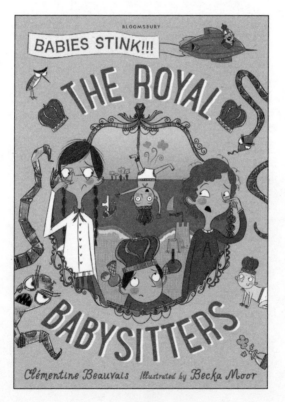

Available now

WILL THIS BE THE WORST WEDDING EVER?
Join Holly, Anna and Pepino
on their second adventure

Available now